Antarctic
prion

Wilson's storm petrel

Emperor
penguin

Southern giant petrel

Snowy
sheathbill

Macaroni penguin

Kelp gull

Antarctic
tern

Black-browed
albatross

Imperial shag

South polar skua

One Day on Our Blue Planet... in the Antarctic © Flying Eye Books 2016.

This is a first edition published in 2016 by Flying Eye Books,
an imprint of Nobrow Ltd. 62 Great Eastern Street, London, EC2A 3QR.

All characters, illustrations and text © Ella Bailey 2016.
Ella Bailey has asserted her right under the Copyright, Designs
and Patents Act, 1988, to be identified as the Author of this Work.

Published in the US by Nobrow (US) Inc.
Printed in Latvia on FSC assured paper.

ISBN: 978-1-909263-67-3

Order from www.flyingeyebooks.com

Ella Bailey

ONE DAY

✵————◦ ON OUR ◦————✵

BLUE PLANET

...IN THE ANTARCTIC

Flying Eye Books

London – New York

As day breaks on the Antarctic continent an
Adélie penguin chick waddles along the frozen coast.

She weaves her way across the nesting grounds,

to where her parents are calling for her.

Now she is old enough, this little penguin will head out
into the vast Antarctic ocean. Her mother feeds her one last meal,

before she sets out across the ice. She passes emperor
penguins heading inland to their own nesting grounds...

...until, finally, she reaches the water's edge.

There is nothing left to do except...

...jump!

She cannot fly, but in the water she is as swift and as graceful as any bird in the sky.

Her streamlined shape makes her an excellent swimmer.
She travels many, many miles each day in search of food...

...through the open southern waters where giants swim...

...and deep under the ice where a colourful world lies hidden.

Here she finds plenty of krill, fish and squid to eat...

...but she has to avoid becoming **food** herself!

Phew a narrow escape!

She heads further north
where she discovers fur seals

and strange
colourful penguins.

It may be many years before this young chick returns to solid land. Until then, her thick layer of fat keeps her warm throughout the short winter days...

...and during the long, bitter cold nights, where she rests on floating ice, until a new sun rises, on another day on our blue planet.

UNDER THE ICE IN
THE ANTARCTIC

Orca

Antarctic
fur seal

Antarctic
krill

Leopard seal

Antarctic
silverfish

Crabeater seal

Arnoux's beaked whale

Glacial
squid

Antarctic minke whale

Hourglass dolphin